THE THERAPIST SECRET

The D.L. Series

Kimberly Moses

REJOICE
Essential Publishing

Kimberly Moses/Rejoice Essential Publishing

PO BOX 512

Effingham, SC 29541

www.republishing.org

Unless otherwise indicated, scripture is taken from the King James Version.'

The Therapist Secret/Kimberly Moses

ISBN-13: 978-1-956775-06-8

Library of Congress Control: 2021951221

CONTENTS

PREFACE

I made a choice to tell my truth. It's my mess that God turned into a message. I refused to allow the enemy to cause me shame. I told God that I would start saying my testimony more. It's the story of how I was delivered out of homosexuality, which caused me to lose everything. As I wrote some of the pages, I wept as the Spirit of God came upon me and gave me the words to type. Some parts of this book have been fictionalized to protect the identity of others. I struggled through writing certain parts because I never talked about it before. However, I leaned into God for strength and received courage and even more importantly, deliverance. My prayer is for the reader to get deliverance as well. Please sow this book into someone's life who is bound. May God's power set them free through this book.

This is part 2 of the D.L. Series.

THE BIG DAY

It was 6 am and Veronica woke up. She had decided to sleep on the couch in her one-bedroom apartment. Her apartment was small and was infested with ants, mice, among other different insects and located in the hood. The hallway smelled like marijuana and the sounds of people arguing often penetrated the thin walls. Veronica grew weary and always found herself constantly praying to stay encouraged. She knew one day that her life would be restored. She had endured many hardships and couldn't believe she was in such an awful place. She didn't have a lot of money and had to get food from a local food bank.

She was a beautiful African American woman. Her skin was radiant and her hair was dyed honey blonde. She was single and desired to be remarried. No one knew the pain that she carried inside. She seemed to have everything together. She battled depression even though she was called to minister full time.

When Veronica opened up her eyes, she felt some discomfort in her back. "Man, sleeping on this couch really hurts my back. Something has to change," she thought. Her options were limited. She often chose to sleep on the small loveseat and curl up in a ball because she couldn't stretch out due to a lack of room. She was given a mattress and a bed frame by a pastor who felt sorry for her because there was no furniture in the apartment. However, the mattress sunk in the middle and springs were poking through. When Veronica decided to lay in the bed, she would sleep on the edge on the firmest parts of the mattress.

Veronica slept on air mattresses for almost two years, so she was grateful to have a bed. Even though her life was hard naturally, she was thriving in the spirit. She had a radical encounter with God and her life was never the same. One day she fell on her face when receiving some devastating news and cried out to God for help. She started to feel His presence and hear His voice. Then she knew He was real. As a result, she started to preach and doors started to open.

"What time is it?" she said out loud. She reached for her phone on the coffee table and saw that it was

6 am. She was scheduled to preach at the local church she attended in a couple of hours. When she grabbed her phone, she checked her notifications and came across some alerts from her ministry website. The email said the following:

Veronica Hawthorne Ministries has received the following comments on the home page. Anonymous has posted "Pussy eater." Girl4Life has posted, "She eats pussy and is not who she says she is."

When Veronica's eyes read these comments, she sat straight up on the couch. Panic rushed through her. "Oh no. I have to delete these comments before someone sees this. I hope these nasty comments weren't on my site for long," she thought.

Veronica tried to delete the comments from her phone, but the website wouldn't allow her to do it. She jumped off the couch and rushed into her bedroom to get her laptop. She logged into the computer and was able to delete the comments.

"This girl just won't go away," she exclaimed. "I have to preach this morning and the enemy is trying to get me upset. Lord, help me."

Veronica knew Sandra, one of her ex-lovers, wrote the comments on her website. "Sandra and her new girlfriend must have written the comments together," she thought. Sandra had tried for months to reconcile with Veronica but was unsuccessful. Veronica was now saved and on fire for God. She knew that homosexuality was an abomination in God's sight. After months without communication, Sandra wanted to reconnect with Veronica. When Veronica first got saved, Sandra tried to pretend to have a relationship with God just to gain reentrance into her life. However, she just wanted Veronica.

Veronica decided to put distance between her and Sandra. She blocked her from her phone and social media. Her actions infuriated Sandra. Veronica even had to place a restraining order on Sandra, but that didn't stop her from reaching out. Over time, Sandra reached out to mutual friends to message Veronica. Sending messages like, "I miss you. Can we talk? Guess what happened? I won't try anything. I just want to keep our friendship." Veronica didn't want to get sucked back into a relationship with Sandra, so she blocked the mutual friends as well. As a result, Sandra became bitter and sought revenge.

"I may have eaten coochie before, but I will never do it again. I'm a new creature in Christ and the old man has passed away," Veronica exclaimed into the atmosphere.

She thought it was ironic that the enemy would use these tactics to bring up her past on the same day that she was to preach and share her testimony publicly for the first time of her deliverance.

"I will not be ashamed. God, help me to be bold because You have done a glorious work," she prayed.

Veronica jumped into the shower, then when finished, she put a towel around her as she stood in front of the mirror. She brushed her pearly white teeth. Her smile would light up a room and was like a breath of fresh air. People would often tell her that the joy of the Lord could be seen when she smiled.

As she stared into the mirror, nervousness kicked in. Veronica exhaled, "You got this."

"God must be doing something powerful today because the enemy is trying to put fear on me," Veronica thought.

Veronica went to her closet and picked out a beautiful dress that accentuated her shape, but still considered modest. The dress wasn't too revealing but relatively high fashion. Since she had to stand in front of the church today and speak, Veronica wanted to look her best.

She put on her undergarments, lotion, deodorant, dress, stockings, and high heels and sits down on the floor in front of a long body mirror to do her makeup and hair. She knew that her living situation was only temporary and one day, she would have some nice furniture.

Veronica got into her car that was visibly damaged by hail and drove to church. She was embarrassed often because people would stop and stare at her once totaled car. They couldn't believe the many dents that they saw. The hail storm had put over 200 dents onto the small black Nissan. However, Veronica swallowed her pride and got the car because it had low mileage and she needed a reliable car. Soon after buying it, she found out that the car wasn't as dependable as she thought.

One snowy day in Colorado Springs, Veronica got into her car and it wouldn't start. She didn't have any help, so she began to walk to church, crying and praying. She couldn't afford to fix her car. When she went to church, people came up to her and comforted her. They asked what was wrong and when they found out, they helped her with it. They raised an offering of $200. A nice couple took her home, jumped the car, and then took her to a shop to get a brand-new battery.

Veronica pulled up to the church and walked inside. She greeted people as she made her way to the front. The service was starting soon. She took a seat on the front pew and exhaled.

"Everything is going to work out," she told herself.

At that moment, a lady got the microphone and opened up in prayer. Next, the choir sang a few songs and the pastor made some announcements.

"Today, we have a special speaker. Sister Veronica, who is doing extraordinary things for the Lord, and will share her testimony. I prayed and God instructed me to have her speak this morning," Pastor Joe said. The church said in unison, "Amen."

Pastor Joe was an elderly man who suffered many hardships. He recently had undergone hip surgery and a week later, he was back at the church trying his best to run things. The staff and his wife scolded him to rest, but the Pastor was resistant. Miraculously he no longer needed to use the walker to support him. Because God healed him, he had a swift recovery.

"Okay, sister Veronica you're up," Pastor said.

As Veronica stood up, the people applauded her and started praising God. As Veronica looked at the faces of the people in the congregation, she gripped the sides of the podium, swallowed, and pushed past the fear. As she spoke, she started to feel the anointing and relaxed.

"Today is the first day that I fully share my testimony. It is hard for me. When I woke up this morning, there were hate messages on my website about what I will share with you today. I know God will do something powerful today because the enemy is trying to fight me, but the devil is defeated and Jesus is Lord. You are looking at a woman who lost everything and hit rock bottom due to sexual sin, perversion, disobedience, selfishness, and rebellion."

At that moment, tears began to fill the corner of Veronica's eyes and her voice started to crack as she felt the urge to sob. She paused and took a deep breath.

"That's alright. Take your time. Touch her Lord," the people prayed and encouraged her from the pews.

Veronica replied, "Thank you. I was on top of the world and had everything anybody could have wanted until…."

CHAPTER 2

SEXUAL DYSFUNCTION

It was a sunny day and Veronica was in the bedroom of the five-bedroom house she shared with her husband.

"Hmmm. Roger has been upstairs in his man cave for a while." She thought, "he is about to be deployed overseas for six months. Let me put on something sexy and go make love to my husband."

Roger's man cave was the bonus room upstairs. He had lots of books, video games, a big-screen television, and a futon. Roger spent many hours upstairs and sometimes Veronica would go up there to spend time with him. Once, she caught Roger looking at porn on his computer. This particular time, she quietly tip-toed up the stairs and when she peeked around the staircase, she saw exactly what Roger was engaging in. She exclaimed, "I caught you!"

Roger slammed his laptop shut to hide his actions. "No, you didn't. What are you talking about?" Roger lied. He was embarrassed because his darkest secret had been exposed. "I was looking at some children's toys," he yelled.

"Stop lying to me. I saw you looking at someone sucking someone's penis. Just tell the truth," Veronica shouted back, hurting because of her husband's behavior. "You must think I'm stupid," she snarled.

Roger stood there stunned in the front of his futon and Veronica stomped downstairs. "No wonder he can't last long. He has been up here masturbating every night," she thought. Pornography had really taken a toll on their marriage. Roger later confessed and explained that he couldn't last long because masturbating compromised his longevity.

Today the thoughts of Roger's upcoming deployment were racing in her mind as she searched through her lingerie drawer. She chose a light lilac lacy teddy and matching G-string.

"I know Roger will love this," she said to herself as she changed into the lingerie. Before she headed upstairs into her husband's man cave, she checked herself in the full body mirror hanging in her closet. She wanted to make sure everything was perfect and that Roger would be stimulated when he laid eyes on her.

"Oh yes!" she whispered as she noticed the teddy accentuating all her curves. She went upstairs and Roger was sitting on the futon. He looked at Veronica, but his response wasn't what she expected. Roger starred right through Veronica and wasn't turned on at all by her outfit. Veronica swallowed her pride and sat next to Roger.

"So, I get no response?" she asked.

"In a minute," he replied. Roger was caught up in watching some sport's commentary.

Veronica waited for about five minutes and longed for her husband's affection before she grew impatient. She grabbed the remote and cut the TV off.

"This can be watched later on the DVR. Right now, we need to make love and get it in all we can before you deploy for six months," Veronica said.

"You're right," Roger said, laying back on the futon.

"I hope you like this outfit," Veronica said, fishing for compliments.

"Oh yeah," Roger said half-heartedly.

Veronica straddled Roger and leaned forward to kiss him. The two locked lips but there was one problem. Roger's mind was elsewhere and he couldn't get aroused.

"Ugh," Veronica sighed as she hopped off her husband.

"I'm sorry. We will do it later. I promise," Roger reassured his wife.

Veronica frowned as she walked down the stairs disappointedly. "I put on this outfit for nothing!" she thought. She took off the lingerie and placed it into her drawer. Then she changed into a t-shirt and jeans.

Veronica wanted to bond with her husband but instead she decided to call her best friend, Jackie. She and Jackie were like sisters and have known each other since middle school. Veronica just needed to vent and lay some of her burdens on her friend. She walked outside onto the deck and had a seat. She knew she would have privacy and Roger wouldn't hear her conversation there. Veronica picked up her cell phone and called Jackie.

"Hey girl! What's going on?" Jackie exclaimed.

"Nothing. Just at the house... bored," Veronica said.

"Well, we can go to the mall and do some shopping," Jackie said.

"Nah. I just want to stay here at the house and spend time with Roger before he deploys," Veronica said.

"Oh yeah. How's that going?" Jackie asked.

"Not good. Honestly, I am so bored with my sex life," Veronica confessed.

"What!" Jackie exclaimed.

"I've been married to Roger for eight years and I have never had an orgasm. I want to experience that. He only wants to do the missionary position. He won't perform oral sex on me because he says that only lesbians do that to each other. I can't even get wet half the time. I had to go to the store and purchase some KY jelly. Once I even fell asleep during sex and sometimes, I get so upset because Roger only lasts for two minutes or so and I am left hanging," Veronica vented.

"Wow. I didn't know you felt like this," Jackie inquired.

"I'm sorry to let you into my bedroom, but you know me. I know I can trust you and you will give me some sound advice," Veronica said.

"Most definitely. Well, have you tried talking to him?" Jackie asked.

"Yes, but he hasn't changed," Veronica said.

"Really?" said Jackie.

"Yes. I even put lingerie on sometimes and he acts as if I am invisible," Veronica said sadly.

"Keep trying to reconnect. Perhaps play a sex board game. My man and I do it all the time. We are like rabbits," Jackie said in laughter.

Veronica chuckles. "Girl, you are crazy."

"Seriously, the game works. Go to that 'His and Her's store up the street. They have all kinds of freaky things to spice up your marriage there. Trust me. You will thank me later," Jackie stated as she smiled on the other end of the phone.

"Alright. I'll go pick up a game. I'll let you know how everything works out," Veronica said reluctantly.

"Please do," Jackie said.

"Ok. Well, let me go. I am going to spend some time with Roger. I love you. Bye," said Veronica.

"Love you more. Bye-bye," Jackie said.

The two friends disconnected. Veronica went back into the house and up to Roger's man cave. She sat next to her husband, pretending to enjoy his company. However, her mind was miles away.

"Sex board games? Is my husband attracted to me? Am I overthinking this intimacy thing with him?"

Her mind raced so much that she had to excuse herself.

"Hunny, I will be back later. I am going downstairs to watch one of my reality shows as I cook dinner," Veronica said.

Roger reaches out and grabs his wife's hand.

"Okay. Don't worry. I'll promise I will take care of you later," Roger said, as he caressed his wife's hand.

Veronica smiled and Roger let go of her hand as she left the room. While downstairs, Veronica turned on her tablet to watch the "Bad Feisty Women's Club." This reality show was full of lesbianism, fights, cursing, partying, sex, and drama. Veronica enjoyed watching shows like this because she felt it spiced up her boring life.

Veronica propped up the tablet on the kitchen island and pulled out the items to make a salad. As she chopped the vegetables, something in the episode stuck out - the women chatting about performing oral sex on each other.

"Do you eat box?" a voice said on the show.

"Yes," another lady answered.

At that moment, the idea of having oral sex performed on her consumed her thoughts. She didn't realize that a seed of perversion was being planted.

"My husband has never gone down on me," she thought as she continued to chop. After the salad was made, Veronica took out the marinated chicken breasts and put them on the griddle. Roger and Veronica loved to eat healthy foods and they enjoyed trying new foods together. Food is what kept them together all those years. It was over a hot meal, where they had some of the best conversations and Veronica seemed to have Roger's full attention. She did not have to compete with sports at the dinner table.

"Well, everything with Roger isn't bad. He is a great provider but a lousy lover," she thought. "I guess I can't have everything."

It was now dinner time, and Roger smiled at his wife. He complimented her cooking and when they were done eating, he cleared the table. He took his wife into the bedroom by grabbing her hand and led the way. The two kissed passionately and undressed. The sex was over as soon as it began. Roger climaxed, but Veronica did not. Instead, she smiled as if she was satisfied and kissed her husband. The two dozed off into a deep sleep.

The next day, Roger was busy being processed to prepare for deployment. He had to fill out lots of paperwork, get some vaccines and other shots. While Roger was away, Veronica couldn't get Jackie's advice out of her head.

"Sex Board Game!"

Veronica decided to go to the 'His and Her' shop. "I will invest in my marriage," she thought. As she entered the store, she had no idea that she was being watched. Sandra was checking her out from behind a clothing rack. Even though Sandra was naturally beautiful, she didn't flaunt it. She wanted to look hard and masculine. She cut her hair into a fade and dressed as a man.

"I have to do something to break the ice," Sandra thought. She walked over to Veronica and decided to offer help.

"Do you need help finding anything?" she asked.

"No," Veronica said. She was embarrassed and didn't want anyone to know what she was going to buy.

"Well. My name is Sandra. Let me know if you need help," Sandra said and proceeded to walk away.

Veronica nodded but immediately began to feel overwhelmed by the wide selection in the store. She just wanted to hurry up and get home.

"Ummm. I changed my mind. I do need help. Can you tell me where the sex board games are located?" Veronica said.

"Right this way," Sandra said as she walked towards the board games. Sandra hung out in this store often, so she was knowledgeable of where things were located.

"Thank you," Veronica said. She saw the games and picked up the first one she saw, then purchased it. She felt as if someone was watching her. She had no idea how right she was. As Veronica left the store, Sandra also walked out, hopped into her car, and followed Veronica home.

"You will be mine," Sandra whispered underneath her breath as she stalked Veronica.

Veronica had no idea that she was being followed. She just wanted to get home and try the game with her husband. She desired to experience an orgasm. She pulled up to her house, got out of the car and walked inside. Sandra parked her car up the street from

Veronica's home so as to not be noticed. She now knew where Veronica lived and she started scheming on how to gain access into her life.

Later that night, Veronica called Roger downstairs.

"Babe, I have a surprise for you," she said.

"What?" Roger asked as he entered the room.

Veronica pulled the sex board game out of the plastic bag. She opened it up and it sparked Roger's interest. The two enjoyed a hot and steamy experience so much that they couldn't finish the board game.

Roger and Veronica made love throughout the night. During the intimacy, Veronica realized just how right Jackie had been. She planned to call her the next day to tell her all the details.

CHAPTER 3

OVERCOME BY LUST

It was the day of Roger's Deployment and Veronica tried her best not to cry. She was going to miss her husband. For six long months, she would have to sleep alone. She would have only the memories of her husband's kisses on her soft skin. Veronica made a light breakfast of scrambled eggs, crispy bacon, toast with strawberry jam, and fresh-squeezed orange juice. Over the meal, Veronica and Roger stared into each other's eyes and enjoyed each other's company before it was time to go to the airport.

It was almost 9 am and Roger had to report to his commander to be cleared to fly out. Roger placed his bags into the car then Veronica drove her husband to the airport.

"I am going to miss you, Babe," said Veronica.

"I am going to miss you too. I will call you as soon as I can," Roger said.

Veronica pulls up to the airport, parks the car, and gets out to hug her husband. Roger gets his bags out of the trunk and sits them on the curb. He looks at his wife with a sense of dread because he doesn't want to leave her. He pecks her mouth then hugs her as long as he can.

"Bye, Honey," Roger said.

"Bye, Babe," Veronica replied. She gets inside of her car, drives off, and many thoughts begin to flood her mind.

"What am I going to do with my spare time? Should I join a gym, write a book, or learn new recipes? I hope this deployment goes by fast."

Before Veronica knew it, she was pulling back into her driveway. Time had flown by. She had no idea that Sandra was parked down the street watching her every move.

The next day, Veronica had to work at the clinic. She was a physical therapist and enjoyed working with patients. Her biggest joy was to see people recuperate and get back on their feet. As Veronica prepared to go to work, she pulled her hair back into a bun. Then she put on some scrubs and work shoes, which made her feet feel like she was walking on clouds. Veronica did one last check of her appearance in the mirror, nodded her head in approval before she dashed out the door and jumped into her car. As Veronica pulled off, Sandra followed her. Sandra made sure that there was enough distance because she didn't want Veronica to get spooked.

She noticed that Veronica parked at Walterboro Outpatient Clinic and went inside. Sandra finds a parking spot and stares at the door, she says, "So this is where you work." Sandra knew she had to be employed there so she could gain access to Veronica's life.

Sandra went home to her apartment. She researched employment opportunities at Walterboro Outpatient Clinic on the internet and noticed that they were hiring. She didn't have many skills but knew she could clean the gym and other rooms, so she applied for the maintenance job. Sandra knew that for her plan to work, she would have to be patient.

A week had passed, Roger was able to video chat with his wife. However, the two didn't talk long. Their conversations were short and sweet. Veronica had no idea that Roger had made a new friend, Sergeant Brown, an attractive woman. Sergeant Brown took a liking to Roger and she wanted to spend every moment with him. Roger felt an attraction for her as well. They walked the military base and went to the chow hall together. Roger even rushed his conversations with his wife because Sergeant Brown was somewhere near.

One night, as Roger was sitting on the steps outside his barracks, Sergeant Brown came to sit beside him. The two looked into each other's eyes and their lips brushed. Roger pulled back because he knew he could get into trouble for having an affair. He was aroused and his eyes looked down at his crotch. Sergeant Brown followed his eyes and noticed his erection through his pants. Her head immediately lowered towards his pelvic area, but Roger stopped her.

"I can't let you do this," he said. Then he walked away and Sergeant Brown didn't bother to follow. Roger went into his room, locked the door, and prayed.

"Lord, I almost cheated on my wife tonight. Please help me not to sin against you. I love my wife, but my eyes sometimes wander. I repent, Lord."

Throughout the deployment, Roger avoided Sergeant Brown because he found her to be very beautiful. He knew that his flesh was weak and he didn't want to set himself up for failure. Eventually, she left Roger alone, especially after the time when he yelled at her after swallowing the choking reality that his marriage really was in trouble.

"Leave me alone! I love my wife! I am not interested in you. Not now. Not ever!" he shouted after Sergeant Brown tried to walk with him to the chow hall.

Sergeant Brown looked hurt and stood speechless as Roger walked away. She didn't understand how things turned so fast. He was into her weeks ago and now he didn't want anything to do with her.

Meanwhile, in the States, Sandra's plan was beginning to take off. She aced her interview and was hired as a maintenance worker at Walterboro Outpatient Clinic. On her first day on the job, she ran into Veronica, treating a patient in the gym. After the patient was rolled away in the wheelchair and Veronica was writing on her clipboard, and Sandra decided to make her move.

"Hey. I know you," she said as she approached Veronica.

"Hey…," Veronica said as she tried to figure out how she knew her in return. "Oh no," Veronica said as she remembered where the lady knew her from.

"Don't worry. It's our secret," Sandra said as she smiled.

Veronica smiled back nervously and said, "I thought you worked there." She made sure she didn't say the name of the 'His and Her' shop.

"I used to, but now I work here," Sandra replied. "I didn't mean to make you feel some kind of way. I just wanted to introduce myself. I'm Sandra."

"It's okay. I'm Veronica."

"It was nice seeing you," Sandra said as she walked away.

"You too," Veronica replied.

For weeks as the two women worked, they kept running into each other. They would smile and speak. Over time, the small talk grew and Sandra knew she was gaining entry into Veronica's life.

One day after Veronica finished up with a patient in the gym, Sandra walked in with her cleaning supplies. The two women started to engage in a conversation.

"Do you have any children," Sandra inquired.

"No. Do you?" Veronica asked.

"No. My puppy is my kid," Sandra said, then chuckled.

"What kind of dog do you have," Veronica asked while smiling.

"A poodle," Sandra replied.

"They are super cute," Veronica said.

Sandra knew this was her moment to get in personal contact with Veronica.

"We should hang out so you can meet my poodle. You will love her. You should call me sometimes.

Let me key in my number on your phone," Sandra suggested.

"Okay," Veronica said while giving Sandra her phone. Veronica was glad that the conversation with Sandra wasn't awkward and was glad to have a new friend since Roger was away.

Sandra typed her phone number into Veronica's phone and called herself. When the phone rang, she hung it up. Veronica had no idea of the trap that laid ahead. The two women said goodbye and continued working. Veronica forgot all about saving Sandra's number. However, Sandra didn't forget to save Veronica's number. As soon as she was able, she took her phone out of her pocket and made sure she saved the phone.

"I'm going to put this number to use," Sandra said underneath her breath.

Later that night, Veronica watched her favorite reality show, "Bad Feisty Women's Club." She hadn't heard from Roger in a couple of days. She missed him terribly and was beginning to feel overwhelmingly lonely. Suddenly, she received a text.

"Hey, this is Sandra. What are you up to?"

"Nothing much except watching my favorite show," Veronica replied.

"Oh yeah. What show?" Sandra inquired with the hope that Veronica would keep engaging.

"Bad Feisty Women's Club," Veronica typed.

"Really? I love that show! Cookie is a mess," Sandra texted.

"Girl. yes," Veronica said.

"My favorite is Amber because we have a lot in common," Sandra replied, wanting desperately for the conversation to continue.

"Omg! How so?" Veronica asked.

"Well, if I tell you, don't judge me. You have to promise," Sandra typed, baiting her further.

Veronica's interests were sparked. She had no idea what she was about to find out.

"I promise," Veronica texted.

"I like to eat box," Sandra said, full force on the direct button.

Veronica was a bit taken back. She really didn't know what to say. She remembers how she desired Roger to perform oral sex on her. She wanted to know how it felt. She loved her husband and didn't want to entertain anyone else.

"Well, to each its own. We all have different things we like to do," she replied.

"I'm sorry for putting it all out there. I just felt like sharing that," Sandra typed. She was fishing to see if Veronica was still interested.

"I didn't know you like women," Veronica typed.

"Well truthfully, I like you," Sandra typed, trying to get into Veronica's head.

"I'm married," Veronica responded.

"Please forgive me. I had no idea," Sandra lied.

"I forgive you. I don't wear my ring when I work," Veronica said.

"If you never want to talk to me again, I understand," Sandra responded.

"No, you are okay," Veronica replied.

"So we can be friends," Sandra replied.

"Yes," typed Veronica.

Sandra typed a smiley face.

"I am going to eat something and go to bed. I'm exhausted. TTYL," Veronica replied.

Then Sandra typed, "TTYL."

Veronica stood in disbelief. She couldn't believe that another woman hit on her. Curiosity plagued her mind, but she shook off the thoughts. She cut the television off and went to bed early.

A few days went by and Veronica and Sandra spoke more at work and texted more throughout the day. Eventually, Veronica couldn't resist Sandra's flirtations. She decided that while her husband was away, she would explore her curiosity. Veronica was sitting in the parking lot at work when the spirit of lust entered her. She felt the intensity of the lust entering her soul. Immediately, she was burning hot with desire. She picked up her phone to text Sandra.

"Hey. I remember you told me that you like to eat box. Can you come over tonight?"

"Oh wee! Are you sure?" Sandra replied with an added heart emoji.

"Yes. Here is my address," Veronica sent her address.

She had no idea that Sandra had been stalking her for weeks.

After sending the text, she sat in disbelief. She couldn't take back the text. She tried to justify her actions so she wouldn't feel so bad.

"Well, Roger won't do it for me. He will never know," Veronica said to herself.

Later that night, Veronica took a hot bath. She put on a teddy and waited on the couch. She heard a knock on the door. She opened the door and she saw Sandra's eyes light up. The two women went straight to the bedroom and Sandra performed oral sex on Veronica.

Yes, Veronica reached a climax but she was deceived of the spiritual consequences. While she was engaging in sexual activity, a transfer of spirits occurred. She didn't know the demons Sandra battled. Hell now had its grip on Veronica's life.

CHAPTER 4

THE CONFLICT

The next day after the sexual encounter with Sandra, Veronica laid in bed trying to process everything. Roger never made her climax and she was shocked that a woman could. She managed to shake off any guilt of her infidelity and picked up the phone to text Sandra who had left a few hours ago.

"I enjoyed it. I wouldn't mind doing it again," Veronica texted.

Sandra sent a heart emoji.

Veronica was different. She wasn't aware of the darkness following her. Veronica showered, dressed, then grabbed a bagel. She had to tell someone what was going on. She picked up the phone and called Jackie.

"Hello," Jackie said.

"Hey. I have something to tell you. Please don't be mad," Veronica pleaded.

"Ok," Jackie said in anticipation.

"I slept with a woman," Veronica said nervously.

"You did what!" Jackie exclaimed.

"I know. I know! I'm so stupid," Veronica said with her hand on her forehead.

"What happened?" Jackie asked.

"Well, you know Roger never performed oral sex on me because he said only lesbians do that. I would watch Bad Feisty Women's Club and they would always talk about eating box. I would always wonder how it would feel. So I met this woman at the 'His and Her' store one night - back when you told me to get the sex board game. This same woman started working with me. Weeks went by and we started a friendship. She came onto me and told me she likes to eat box. I couldn't get her words out of my head.

So one day, I was overtaken by lust and told her she could eat my box. I invited her over and it happened last night," Veronica explained to her.

"Oh my goodness," Jackie laughed in shock.

"Yeah, and the crazy part is that I loved it," Veronica sighed.

"Girl. What are you going to do?" Jackie asked.

"I don't know," Veronica said.

"Well, you have to stop and let this be a one-time thing. You messed up, but you are married. You have to hold down your home while Roger is away," Jackie said.

"What if I don't want to stop," Veronica asked.

"You will mess up your life. Nothing good comes out of cheating. It doesn't matter if it's with a woman. It's still adultery," Jackie said.

"I knew you would always tell me the truth," Veronica said.

"Of course. I love you," Jackie said.

"I love you too. I'll call you later. I got to go to work," Veronica said and then hung up the phone.

She sighed and appreciated her friend's counsel. Jackie always told her what she needed to hear, not what she wanted to hear.

Veronica got into the car, drove off, and started to eat her bagel. Her drive to work flew by because her mind was in a battle. Should she follow her desire or the sound counsel of her friend? Was having her desire fulfilled worth losing her marriage?

At work, Veronica had a busy schedule. She saw Sandra down the hall sweeping but decided to dodge her and went into the bathroom. She wasn't ready to face her yet and still needed to process everything. Veronica hoped that Sandra didn't see her as she disappeared into the restroom. However, Sandra did.

Veronica stood at the sink staring at her reflection. Suddenly Sandra entered the restroom and Veronica was surprised. Before Veronica could say anything, Sandra kissed her, then led her into one of the stalls and locked the door. Sandra pulled down Veronica's pants, kneeled on the floor, and started to perform oral sex on her. Veronica exploded with pleasure but had to keep her voice down.

The two women finished and freshened themselves up before exiting the restroom. No one heard what just happened. They said bye to each other. Veronica couldn't believe she allowed Sandra to do that again.

The next day at work, Veronica decided to avoid Sandra because she was like a drug. She couldn't say no and would melt in her presence. She sat in her car for her break, hoping not to run into Sandra. However, Sandra was following her every move. Sandra went into the parking lot and saw Veronica sitting in her car. She went up to the window and tapped on it. Veronica was stunned but gave in unlocking the door for her, and Sandra hopped in.

"Why are you sitting out here?" Sandra asked.

"I just needed some time to think. I'm starting to feel bad for cheating on my husband." Veronica replied.

"I'm sorry. I am not trying to make you feel bad. I thought you wanted me in that way," Sandra said.

"I know. I am sorry for leading you on," Veronica said.

"I want to tell you something," Sandra said.

"What," Veronica said.

"Years ago, my older cousin and his friends ran a train on me and raped me," Sandra said.

"Oh my goodness," Veronica said in shock.

"Yes. I was fourteen and my parents were out of town. They put my older cousin in charge of watching me. Well, my cousin invited some friends over and they were drinking and doing drugs. They came into my room and raped me. I was sore afterwards and had bruises all over from when they held me down and hit me to prevent me from fighting back. I began to hate all men from that moment," Sandra said.

Veronica started to have empathy for Sandra and decided not to end things with Sandra at that moment.

"That's horrible. I can understand now why you prefer women," Veronica said.

Sandra put her hand on top of Veronica's and the bond between them strengthened. A spark of passion started to be ignited.

"How long is your break?" Sandra asked.

"I got about 20 minutes," Veronica stated.

"That's enough time," Sandra said cunningly.

Veronica knew what she was referring to and became overwhelmed with lust. The two women hopped into the backseat and again continued in their sexual tryst. Afterward, the two women embraced and headed back to work.

After work, Veronica was driving home and felt a dark, gloomy shadow sitting behind her. Fear gripped her chest and she felt as if she couldn't breathe. The overwhelming feeling that something bad was going to happen hung over her. This was the first of many panic attacks that Veronica would have in the days to come. She pulled her car into a parking lot and took some deep breaths.

"Inhale"
"Exhale"
"Inhale"
"Exhale"

Veronica felt her heart racing as she peeped into her backseat to check if anyone was there. She felt as if she wasn't alone like something was following her but she couldn't see with her natural eyes. After a few minutes, Veronica got herself together and said, "I'm losing it!"

When Veronica got home, she skipped dinner. She heard her husband's video chat alert, but she didn't want to talk to him. She showered and went to bed. Jackie's words echoed in her mind.

"You committed adultery."

Veronica drifted off to sleep but was startled awake by a dark presence in her room. Veronica gasped and sat straight up in bed in terror. An evil spirit loomed in her room. Her heart throbbed intensely. Immediately, Veronica cut on the lamp at her bedside. She hadn't had a nightmare in a long time and wondered if her cheating on Roger had something to do with it.

Veronica laid in bed for about 20 minutes before she drifted back to sleep. However, she didn't sleep long. No sooner had she drifted back to sleep, she felt a paralyzing weight holding her down. She suspected it was an evil spirit from earlier trying to oppress her. Veronica couldn't move and she fought with this spirit for a few minutes before getting free. She was afraid and decided not to go back to sleep. Dawn slowly approached; Veronica knew she had to get ready to work a long shift.

Exhausted, she got out of bed, dressed, and made some coffee. She drank a cup and went to work.

When she got to work, she saw Sandra cleaning up and waved. Sandra waved back and finished cleaning.

Veronica moved sluggishly throughout the day, but pressed through it. She had an hour break before seeing her next patient, so she decided to rest and hopefully nap. She slipped into the locker room but didn't know that Sandra was following her.

"There you are," Sandra said.

"Hey," Veronica replied.

"What's wrong?" Sandra asked.

"I'm tired. I didn't sleep too well last night," Veronica.said.

"Why?" Sandra asked.

"I feel like my demons are catching up to me. I kept feeling something evil," Veronica explained.

"You believe in demons?" Sandra asked.

"Yes, only because I feel them sometimes. I hope you don't think I am crazy, but they were trying to hold me down in my sleep last night," Veronica said.

"No. I don't think you're crazy," Sandra reassured her.

"I believe it's because of me cheating. I don't think we should continue our relationship," Veronica asserted.

"Don't say that. I don't think that's why you didn't sleep last night. I think it's because you are tired from working too many hours," Sandra said.

"I guess," Veronica said reluctantly.

At that moment, Sandra put her hand on Veronica's thigh and started to massage it. Then she started rubbing the back of her neck. She didn't want her relationship with Veronica to end, so she had to seduce her. She could tell Veronica was enjoying her touch. She thought that Veronica would change her mind about breaking things off if she could sleep with her again.

"Well, let me help you relax some," Sandra said before she made her move. She laid Veronica down and performed oral sex on her on the bench. Afterward, Veronica pulled her pants up and glanced at her watch. She couldn't believe she had fallen for Sandra again.

"I still have about 50 minutes left. I could pass out right here," she said.

"Yeah. Set your alarm and lay back and relax," Sandra said and then left the locker room.

Veronica dozed off and when the alarm sounded, she went back to work. As she worked, guilt finally caught up to her.

"I am addicted to Sandra. I have to stop this," she said to herself. She just didn't know the depth of the enemy's stronghold.

CHAPTER 5

THE BATTLE WITH HELL

One day, Veronica was on the verge of a nervous breakdown. It started when she felt too sick to eat. She couldn't eat around her co-workers even though she was starving. Fearing throwing up in public, she would box up her food and eat later when she was alone.

Then, Veronica started to get gassy. She felt stomach issues developing and gas would get trapped in her chest. The pressure built up and made it difficult for her to walk. She would be miserable until she was able to pass gas.

She went to the emergency room because she thought she was having a heart attack. However, the doctor couldn't find anything wrong with her. She had no idea that she was having a spiritual attack. All she knew was that her symptoms were real to her, even if no one understood.

Acid reflux started to worsen and Veronica couldn't lay flat anymore. She found herself taking a bunch of medication and everything she ate caused indigestion. Veronica would have panic attacks almost daily and would have to focus on her breathing because she felt like she was going to die.

She noticed a rapid decline and couldn't function normally. Driving became difficult. She would have panic attacks driving over bridges and couldn't ride in the car with others. Whenever she would meet new people, her heart would race and she felt sick to her stomach. All Veronica wanted to do was be isolated, which was the devil's plan.

To make matters worse, Veronica started to smell. Everywhere she went, she smelled a sour stench. She would shower three times a day, soak in various salts and bath bombs, and wear all types of fragrances. However, nothing worked. Then one day, she noticed that she was smelling the demonic spirits that would torment her in the night.

One more embarrassing thing happened to Veronica. Her breath started to smell like rotten eggs.

She didn't want to talk to many people because of the anxiety and she didn't want them to smell her. Gums and breath mints didn't work. Brushing her teeth to get rid of the smell was a temporary fix.

One day, she looked into the mirror and saw a bunch of white scabs growing on the back of her tonsils. She was terrified. Her throat would constantly hurt and she would suck on cough drops to get relief throughout the day. Sometimes, the tonsil stones would come up out of her throat at the weirdest time, and she would gag because she was disgusted. She visited the doctor and begged for her tonsils to be removed, but the doctor refused.

"We don't take out tonsils anymore," the doctor said.

Disappointed, Veronica learned to live with tonsillitis. She would get Q-tips and pluck the white scabs off her tonsils. She would gag then gargle with pricey mouthwashes to mask the smell.

After another sexual encounter with Sandra, her vaginal area was irritated. She had developed vaginitis due to rubbing her female parts with Sandra's. Veronica had to treat herself for a yeast infection and get some tablets to balance her vaginal PH levels.

Veronica knew that sleeping with Sandra was the reason for her decline.

She was at a breaking point. She attended counseling sessions weekly for anxiety and learned deep breathing relaxation techniques. These worked temporarily, but she was restless.

People began to whisper at work about Sandra's and Veronica's relationship. The secret relationship they once tried to hide came to light. People knew that Veronica was married and they were disappointed by her actions.

One day, Veronica heard some of her co-workers' conversation through the door. As she approached the door, she stood there quietly, listening.

"I can't believe she is cheating on her husband," one nurse said.

"I didn't think she was on the down-low," another therapist said.

"They need to go somewhere and get a room," another nurse said.

Then they all erupted with laughter. Veronica then opened the door and by the look on their faces, they knew she knew they were talking about her. She pretended like she was grabbing some paperwork, then she exited the room.

She was ashamed. She knew they were right. She was a lost soul and wanted a way out but felt like she was in too deep.

CHAPTER 6

THE ATTACK

The nightmares intensified and daily, Veronica was exhausted because she wasn't sleeping well.

One day after work, Veronica came home and laid on the couch. She was too exhausted to change out of her work clothes. While she slept, Roger video called her again and Sandra texted her a few times. When Veronica woke up, it was about 2 am. She decided not to call her husband. She started to feel bad for cheating on him multiple times. She picked up her phone to read some text messages.

"I am so in love with you," Sandra texted at 8:15 pm.

"I want us to be together," Sandra texted at 8:20 pm.

Veronica was starving and put a frozen pizza in the oven. She responded to Sandra.

"I'm married. I enjoyed our time together, but it cannot happen again. It's over. I made a mistake."

Veronica ate her pizza and then she called her husband on the video chat.

"Hey! Where have you been?" Roger asked.

"I have been working double shifts and I'm exhausted. I just needed to do something extra with my time," Veronica lied.

"Oh yeah. Well, I miss you so much, baby," Roger said.

"I miss you too. I can't wait until you come home," Veronica said.

The two caught up about work and the video call ended a few minutes later. Veronica didn't have to go to work today, so she started to clean up her home.

At 8 am, Sandra woke up in her apartment and saw the text from Veronica. Her spirit was crushed.

"No! No! No! You aren't breaking it off with me," she exclaimed.

Sandra was tired of going through various relationships. She felt like Veronica was the prettiest woman she had ever had and she didn't want to lose her. She picked up the phone and texted Veronica.

"I want to see you today."

"It's not going to happen. Please don't contact me anymore. I put in another transfer to work somewhere else. We can never work because I'm married," Veronica replied.

Sandra was hurt and knew her plan of being with Veronica was failing. She did something drastic.

"We will see if you will be with me," Sandra said out loud.

Sandra got on her computer and searched for information on Veronica. She found out that she was married to Roger. She paid fifty dollars to get Roger's background check and his personal information. She got his email and messaged him.

"Hello Roger. My name is Sandra and I am having an affair with your wife. She doesn't love you anymore. She loves me and we are meant to be together. Every day, I am eating her because you refuse to."

Sandra was satisfied that she told Roger the truth. She wanted Roger out of the way so she could have Veronica. She hoped that her message would cause Roger to divorce Veronica.

Hours went by before Roger saw the email from Sandra. When he first read the message, he thought it was some kind of joke.

"Nah. Veronica wouldn't cheat on me. She is a good girl," he said to himself. Then he got on his video call app and called his wife.

"Hey babe," Veronica said as she smiled at Roger.

However, Roger didn't smile.

"What's wrong?" Veronica asked.

"Babe, I got this really strange email. I want to read it to you," Roger replied.

"Ok," Veronica said.

"Hello Roger. My name is Sandra and I am having an affair with your wife. She doesn't love you anymore. She loves me and we are meant to be together. Every day, I am eating her because you refuse to," he read.

As Roger started reading, Veronica's heart sank into her stomach and she tasted bile in the back of her throat. She knew she was caught. "I am going to kill her," Veronica said in her mind.

"Well, what do you have to say? Is this a joke?" he asked.

"No. Some of its truth," Veronica said. She was embarrassed.

"Huh? What! Did you cheat on me?" Roger asked.

"It happened last week and it was a one-time thing," she lied.

"Wow! So you cheated on me with a woman? How can I compete with that?" Roger asked.

"I am so sorry. I ended it," Veronica said.

"But why? I thought we were happy?" Roger asked.

"I begged you for six years for oral sex, but you refused. I would perform it on you, but you would never do it to me. You would climax and only last two minutes. I never had an orgasm with you," Veronica explained.

"Wow! You are so selfish! You were willing to throw your whole marriage away for your lustful desires!" he yelled.

Veronica was shunned and felt a wave of mixed emotions. She really didn't have the right words to say except, "I'm sorry. Please forgive me."

"I am done," Roger said and ended the call.

Veronica tried to video chat Roger several times, but he wouldn't answer. Veronica just fell on her knees and wept.

"How could I be so stupid?" she said.

After Roger ended the call, he paced the floor. He felt sick to his stomach and he was upset. He replied to Sandra's email. Then he blocked her email address.

"Thank you for telling me the truth, but stay away from my wife. She will never be with you. Don't message me again!"

Roger was hurt and he felt emasculated. All the while, he was trying to make sense out of the situation.

"I could see if she cheated with a man but another woman? I can't compare to a woman," he said as he paced the floor. He ended up cutting his computer off because Veronica kept calling. He wasn't ready to speak with her.

Back in the States, Sandra received the email from Roger and became irate. She replied back but didn't know she was blocked.

"Don't mess with me little boy! I came to get what's mine!" she typed and sent the message.

Sandra was infuriated, so she jumped into the car and drove to Veronica's house. When she arrived, she rang the doorbell.

"Who is it?" Veronica asked, then peeped through the peephole.

"Sandra"

"Go away! I told you we were over," Veronica said.

"I just want to talk," Sandra said.

Veronica ignored her. Sandra ended up banging on Veronica's door for several minutes. She banged so hard, she put a few holes in the front door. Finally, she gave up and went into her car. When she got behind the wheel, she screamed, and her fists hit the steering wheel a few times. She drove off in a fury.

The next day, Veronica had to go to work. As she opened the front door she noticed the holes.

"She will have to pay for this," Veronica exclaimed. She didn't have time to report it because she had to be at work in 30 minutes.

"I'll report this on my lunch break," she said.

When Veronica went to work, she passed Sandra in the hallway. Sandra followed her as she passed.

"I need to talk with you," Sandra said.

"I don't have anything to say to you," Veronica said.

Sandra started to get loud and people started to look. "I need you to listen!" she said.

Veronica shook her head and walked away. She didn't want to make a scene.

Throughout the day, Veronica was able to avoid Sandra. She would peek around the corner and when she saw Sandra, she would walk another way. She would end a session early with a patient, so she wouldn't be found when Sandra came looking.

On Veronica's break, she drove to a local diner and reported Sandra. Veronica spoke with Detective Marlow. When she went back to work, she spoke to her supervisor and asked to work an alternate schedule to make sure she avoided Sandra.

Sandra was hurt but determined to get Veronica back. The next day, she was served paperwork. One was a claim to fix the front door, and the other was a restraining order to stay away from Veronica. Sandra was so upset that she couldn't focus on work. She walked the halls looking for Veronica but couldn't find her. Then she told her supervisor that she wasn't feeling well and left work.

She got in her car and drove straight to Veronica's house. She didn't see her car parked upfront. Sandra parked her car around the corner, then she crept up to the house and jumped the fence. When she was in the backyard, she took a rock and busted a corner of the glass on the backdoor. She made sure that there were no jagged edges before she put her arm through to unlock the door from the other side. She managed to open the door. Then she waited for Veronica to come home.

When Veronica finally arrived home, she was in a broken place. She had tried to call Roger throughout the day, but he still wouldn't take her calls. She decided that she would take a hot bath and go to bed.

When she walked into her front door, the house was very dark. She closed the door behind her, locked it, and proceeded to cut on the light. However, it never happened. Sandra leaped out from the darkness and hit her hard on the head with a lamp.

Veronica passed out. While Veronica was out, Sandra undressed her then bound her hands and feet to the bed. Veronica laid naked, unconscious and when she awoke, Sandra was sexually assaulting her.

"Stop it! Get off me!" Veronica screamed!

"I told you that I wanted to talk," Sandra replied.

Veronica noticed that her hands and feet were bound. She yanked and tried to free herself but to no avail.

"Let me go!" Veronica screamed.

"We were meant to be together," Sandra said.

Veronica moaned in pain. "My head hurts," she said.

"Let me put some ice on it," Sandra said. She went to the kitchen and came back with a Ziplock bag full of ice. Then placed it on Veronica's head.

Veronica cried. She regretted her mistakes. "I got to get out of here or this girl will kill me," she said to herself.

Immediately, she began to do something that she hadn't done in years. She prayed.

"God, if you are real, please get me out of this and I'll serve you," she prayed in her mind.

Sandra continued to violate Veronica until she was satisfied. What used to cause Veronica pleasure now disgusted her. Her fling now became her captor and rapist.

"I wish I never cheated," Veronica thought as she wept. She was sore and swollen from the assault. She laid in agony every time Sandra went down on her. She focused her mind on other things and prayed that it would all be over soon. The circulation in her arms and legs was beginning to go numb. Her limbs were getting numb from hanging and being bound.

A few hours went by and Sandra said, "I'll be back. I'm going to pack up a few of my things and stay with you for a while. Once you show me that you will act right, I'll untie you."

Veronica didn't reply. She laid in pain and fear. Sandra came back and curled up into a fetal position in bed next to Veronica. Then she fell into a deep sleep.

Early the following day, Detective Marlow wanted to check in with Veronica after the report was filed. He called a few times but got no response. So, he and his partner went to the address listed on the report and decided to look around. They knocked on the door but heard no response. They found it odd because Veronica's car was in the front yard.

As they knocked, Sandra and Veronica woke up.

"Knock. Knock. Knock," they heard.

"Help!!!!!!!" Veronica screamed at the top of her lungs.

The detectives heard it.

"Help!!!" Veronica screamed, again. However, Sandra put her hand on top of her mouth and threatened, "Shut up! I will kill you," as she pressed down.

The detectives kicked in the door with their guns positioned to fire.

When Sandra heard the door burst open, she let her hand off Sandra's mouth and opened up the window to escape.

"Help!" Veronica yelled.

They searched the house and cautiously entered the bedroom from where they heard screams emerging.

Sandra managed to open the window by the time they entered, but just as she was about to cross over the window frame, the detectives yelled, "Stop right there or we'll shoot!"

Sandra knew she was caught, so she complied. She surrendered and put her hands up as a sign. One of the detectives went over to her and cuffed her.

Both of the detectives were horrified by what they saw. The other detective grabbed a sheet and put it over Veronica to hide her exposed body. Then he cut the ropes off her hands and feet. Veronica wept violently as she knew that God answered her prayers. Sandra was arrested.

"Would Sandra get out of jail? Would she rape me again?" These thoughts overwhelmed Veronica's mind.

Trembling in fear, Veronica knew she was now on the long road of recovery.

CHAPTER 7

THE CHOICE

Roger got on his computer and he saw an urgent message from Veronica. On the subject line, he saw:

"I was raped!"

His heart dropped and he felt bad for not answering Veronica's calls.

"I wish I was there to protect her," he said to himself.

For weeks, Roger was severely depressed. He couldn't sleep well and the only food he could eat was oatmeal. He lost about ten pounds during that time. He was into Sergeant Brown, but after Veronica confirmed that she was unfaithful, he made it clear that there would never be anything with her. He just wanted to be alone. Getting through his shifts was long and arduous. He had about two more months before coming home.

His first deployment turned out to be a devastating experience. To help cope with his depression, he attended church service held on the military base. One day he was walking and heard some beautiful singing coming from this building. He was drawn in, so he stepped inside and as the choir finished up their song, pastor Rodney came up.

Pastor Rodney was a cook in the military, but he also was a preacher. He wasn't a pastor, but everyone called him one. Pastor Rodney was deployed as well. He was a small man but had a booming voice. When he spoke, he gathered everyone's attention.

Roger heard a wonderful message. This sermon was full of hope and encouragement.

"What should have broken you, didn't kill you, so keep going!", the Preacher exclaimed as Roger took a seat.

"You will laugh again. You will have joy again. It's not hopeless!" Pastor Rodney said powerfully.

"Yes!" Roger said as tears filled his eyes. He needed those words because they were life to him.

"Come to Jesus! Let Him in today! The altar is open. Come up here. Don't hold back!", the preacher said.

Roger felt overwhelmed and couldn't stop weeping. He had so much hatred and pain in his heart. He felt led to go to the altar. He knew it was now or never. He wanted to experience the hope that Pastor Rodney proclaimed. Roger stood up and started to make his way to the front of the church.

People began to clap and Roger knew he was doing the right thing.

"Young man. God's Spirit is all over you. He is ready to deliver you from all the pain that you have been carrying. Will you accept Jesus as your Lord and Savior?"

"Yes I will," Roger sobbed.

Pastor Rodney laid his hand upon Roger and the Spirit of God surged through his body. Roger fell backwards and some men caught him as he laid on his back. They covered Roger with a sheet.

Roger wept on the floor for about 30 minutes. Roger felt a pureness enter his soul. The joy he longed for finally filled him. Suddenly, he heard a voice. "Forgive as I have forgiven you!" He didn't know that it was the voice of God.

The service ended, but he was still on the floor. Pastor Rodney dismissed everyone and stayed with Roger. When Roger came to himself, Pastor Rodney helped him off the floor.

"What happened?" Roger asked.

"The Spirit of God came upon you and you received salvation," Pastor Rodney explained.

"Yes. I heard a voice tell me to forgive as I have forgiven you," Roger said.

"That was God speaking to you. You must obey Him," Pastor Rodney said.

"Ok. I am ashamed to tell you, but I must forgive my wife," Roger said.

"Amen. God will get you through it. I want to explain to you what Romans 10:9 says: If you confess with your mouth and believe in your heart, you shall be saved. Jesus is now the Lord of your life. Please come back tomorrow at 6 pm for Bible Study and we can begin to disciple you to help you on this faith journey." pastor Rodney said.

"Thank you. I will," Roger said. He felt different. He was no longer depressed and wanted to talk to his wife. He entered his room and went to his computer. Then he saw the email from his wife.

"I was raped!"

He called her immediately and his eyes fell in disbelief. A broken Veronica answered the video chat. Her hair was misplaced and her eyes were puffy. Roger's heart broke and tears filled his eyes.

"Roger," Veronica said.

"What happened?" Roger said.

"When I broke things off with Sandra, she broke into the house, hit me on the head with a lamp, tied me to the bed, and raped me over and over again," Veronica cried.

"Where is she now?" Roger said.

"Jail." Veronica replied.

"I wish I were there to protect you," Roger said.

"Me too. I miss you so much," Veronica said.

"Do you have a restraining order?" he asked.

"Yes," she replied.

"I forgive you. I got saved today at church," Roger said.

"Thanks, Babe." Veronica said.

The two continued to chit-chat for a little while longer then called it a night.

Over the next few weeks, Roger continued to pray for his wife and things turned around for him. He was full of peace and his deployment ended quickly. However, things weren't great for Veronica. She struggled to forgive herself for indiscretions.

CHAPTER 8

IT'S OVER

Six months passed and Veronica was now at the airport to pick up Roger. When he got into the car, things were different. He wasn't the loving husband who left six months prior. The two kissed, but there was much distance between the two.

Later that night, the two were intimate, but Roger resented his wife deep down. The tension between them was tangible and totally affected their intimacy. When he looked at Veronica, Roger saw pain. He prayed to forgive her for many months, but he realized that just because he forgave her didn't mean he had to be with her. He struggled to move past the infidelity.

One day after work, Roger came home and Veronica was sitting on the couch. He sat next to her.

"I need to talk to you," Roger said.

"Okay," Veronica said.

"What I am about to say is very difficult and I rehearsed it over and over in my mind. However...I want a divorce," he said.

"What! I thought you had forgiven me?" said Veronica.

"I have, but you broke our trust and defiled our marital bed," Roger said.

"I did apologize and I'm sorry for that," Veronica said.

"I would rather be alone than to live with this pain in my heart," Roger said.

"Don't quit on me. We have so much history together and I love you," Veronica responded.

"I made up my mind. Nothing you say or do will change that. I did try, but this marriage is over," Roger replied.

"Don't say that," Veronica said.

"I'm going to stay at my mom's house for a while until I find a new place to live. Please don't make this more difficult than it has to be," Roger said. He was still hurting and headed out the door.

Veronica got up off the couch to follow him, but Roger quickly got into his car and sped off. Veronica frantically dialed her husband, but he wouldn't answer. That was the last day she ever saw her husband. Her marriage was over and she knew it was her fault.

Things began to swirl out of control for Veronica. The rumors of her affair began to circulate and the supervisor got wind of it. One day at work, Veronica was called into the office.

"The reason why you are here is because of the rumors that are circulating and you had a public fight here." her supervisor stated.

"What rumors? A public fight?" Veronica asked. She pretended she didn't know.

"You had an affair with a woman employed here and sometimes even had sex here. This woman was arrested because of your affair," her supervisor said.

"That's not true. I take my job seriously," Veronica replied.

"We have it on surveillance. Do I need to play the video?" her supervisor asserted.

Veronica knew she was caught and was extremely embarrassed. She shook her head no.

"We have a reputation to uphold. I am sorry, but I have to let you go," her supervisor said.

Veronica was shunned. She couldn't believe she got fired. Hurt, she went to her locker and cleaned it out. On her walk of shame, she walked past the same co-workers who gossiped about her.

"Now they will really have something to talk about," she thought.

Veronica could feel their eyes fixed on her as she walked out of the building. Veronica had no idea what she was going to do. When she got home, she applied for other jobs. Weeks went by and no one contacted her back for employment. Her money was running out and she wasn't able to pay bills.

Veronica needed to do something, so she sought God.

"Lord, I repent for my sins. Thank you for saving me. I want to develop a real relationship with you. Please help me out of this situation and show me how to serve you. Amen."

This prayer was the prayer that changed Veronica's life. A foreclosure sign was eventually put in her front yard, and it caused her to pray more. Miraculously, Roger took over the mortgage, rented it out, and was able to keep the property. Veronica moved into a small apartment. She received a check in the mail and was able to pay off her bills.

One door closed after the others as the Lord redirected Veronica into ministry. She was no longer a physical therapist but a minister of the Lord Jesus Christ.

Now, fast forward, Veronica stood in front of the church, telling her testimony for the first time. People sat on the edge of their chairs as she spoke, anticipating what she would say next.

"You see church, sin equals death. It's not worth sinning against God. For the spirit is willing but the flesh is weak," Veronica said.

"Amen," the church said in unison.

"Sin cost me everything. I lost my marriage. I was raped, shamed, tormented, broken, and bound. Yet, the Lord never gave up on me. He gave me another chance. I am a new creature in Christ, Holy Spirit filled, and fire baptized. I am anointed and purpose-filled. The enemy tried to take me out but failed. Someone here today messed up, and you too, were involved in a same-sex attraction type of relationship. Come to the front so you can receive your deliverance. This message wasn't for everyone, but I know God had me to share for the one. Would you please come forward? I can feel you tugging on my spirit today," Veronica said.

The church went silent and eyes began to look around. Suddenly, a beautiful teenage girl stood up and came to the front. It was apparent that God's Spirit was dealing with her. She began to weep.

Veronica stepped off the podium and stood in front of the girl. She grabbed her hand and the little girl confessed.

"This message was for me today. My mother was praying for me to break things off with this girl I met at school and today I will."

Suddenly, the girl's mother began to shout and weep loudly.

"Lord, I thank You! You heard my prayer! Thank You for saving my baby girl! Oh Lord, I praise You," the mother cried and fell over.

"Someone help the mother up and bring her to the front. We are going to pray," Veronica instructed.

As the mother was brought to the front, a group of elders surrounded her and her daughter.

"Dear Lord, thank You for giving me the courage to share my testimony today because the enemy is overcome by the blood of the Lamb and by the word of our testimony. You drew this young girl here today to hear my deliverance journey. Lord, set her free today. I bind up perversion and cancel the enemy's plans. Lord, loose purity and rip out any same-sex attraction. Remove the wrong person out of her life and bless this young lady to live holy as You are holy. Holy Spirit fall upon her now," Veronica prayed.

The elders were praying in agreement and then Veronica touched the young girl on her forehead. She fell on her knees and out came a growl as deliverance was taking place in her life. When she got up, she shouted, "I've been set free. While I was on the floor, I met the One who died on the cross for me."

COMING SOON

Dante is a highly esteemed professor and married to the principal of the university, Mariah. However, Dante has an internal war occurring when he meets a new student taking his course. Will the truth of his marriage to Mariah come to light? Will Dante betray his wife and lose everything?

Find out what happens in the Professor's Secret.

ABOUT THE AUTHOR

Kimberly Moses started off her ministry as Kimberly Hargraves. She is highly sought after as a prophetic voice, intercessor and prolific author. There is no doubt that she has a global mandate on her life to serve the nations of the world by spreading the Gospel of Jesus Christ. She has a quickly expanding worldwide healing and deliverance ministry. Kimberly Moses wears many hats to fulfill the call God has placed on her life as an entrepreneur over several businesses including her own personal brand Rejoice Essentials which promotes the Gospel of Jesus Christ.

She also serves as a life coach and mentor to many women. She is also the loving mother of two wonderful children. She is married to Tron. Kimberly has dedicated her life to the work of ministry and to serve others under the call God has placed over her life. Kimberly currently resides in South Carolina.

She is a very anointed woman of God who signs, miracles and wonders follow. The miraculous and in-cessant testimonies attributed to her ministry are in-calculable, with many reporting physical and mental healing, financial breakthroughs, debt cancellations and other favorable outcomes. She is known across the globe as a servant who truly labors on behalf of God's people through intercession.

She is the author of The Following:

"Overcoming Difficult Life Experiences with Scriptures and Prayers"
"Overcoming Emotions with Prayers"
"Daily Prayers That Bring Changes"
"In Right Standing,"
"Obedience Is Key,"
"Prayers That Break The Yoke Of The Enemy: A Book Of Declarations,"
"Prayers That Demolish Demonic Strongholds: A Book Of Declarations,"
"Work Smarter. Not Harder. A Book Of Declarations For The Workforce,"
"Set The Captives Free: A Book Of Deliverance."
"Pray More Challenge"

"Walk By Faith: A Daily Devotional"

"Empowering The New Me: Fifty Tips To Becoming A Godly Woman"

"School of the Prophets: A Curriculum For Success"

"8 Keys To Accessing The Supernatural"

"Conquering The Mind: A Daily Devotional"

"Enhancing The Prophetic In You"

"The ABCs of The Prophetic: Prophetic Characteristics"

"Wisdom Is The Principal Thing: A Daily Devotional"

"It Cost Me Everything"

"The Making Of A Prophet: Women Walking in Prophetic Destiny"

"The Art of Meditation: A Daily Devotional"

"Warfare Strategies: Biblical Weapons"

"Becoming A Better You"

"I Almost Died"

<u>"The Pastor's Secret: The D.L. Series"</u>

"June Bug The Busy Bee: The Gamer"

"June Bug The Busy Bee: The Bully"

"The Weary Prophet: Providing Practical Steps For Restoration"

"The Insignificant Woman"

"The Foolish Woman: A Daily Devotional"

"June Bug The Busy Bee: Sibling Rivalry"

"All Things Relationships"

"30 Day Pray For Your Spouse Challenge"

"The Christian Drama Queen Mentality"

"30 Days Praying For The Nations"
"Intercessor's Prayer Notebook"
"Prayer Request Notebook Fervent Effectual Prayers
Of The Righteous"
"The Prophet's Notebook"
"The Photographer's Assistant"
"The Ultimate Entrepreneur"
"Diabetic Caretaker Blood Sugar Log"
"The Preacher's Handbook"
"Christian Weight Loss Journal"
"Couple's Recipe Meal Planner And Notebook"
"Prophetic Dreams And Visions Journal"

You can find more about Kimberly at
www.kimberlyhargraves.com

For Rejoice Essential Magazine, visit
www.rejoiceessential.com

For beauty and t-shirts, visit
www.rejoicingbeauty.com

Please write a review for my books on Amazon.
com

Support this ministry:
Cashapp: $ProphetessKimberly
Paypal.me/remag
Venmo: Kimberly-Moses-19

READ PART ONE

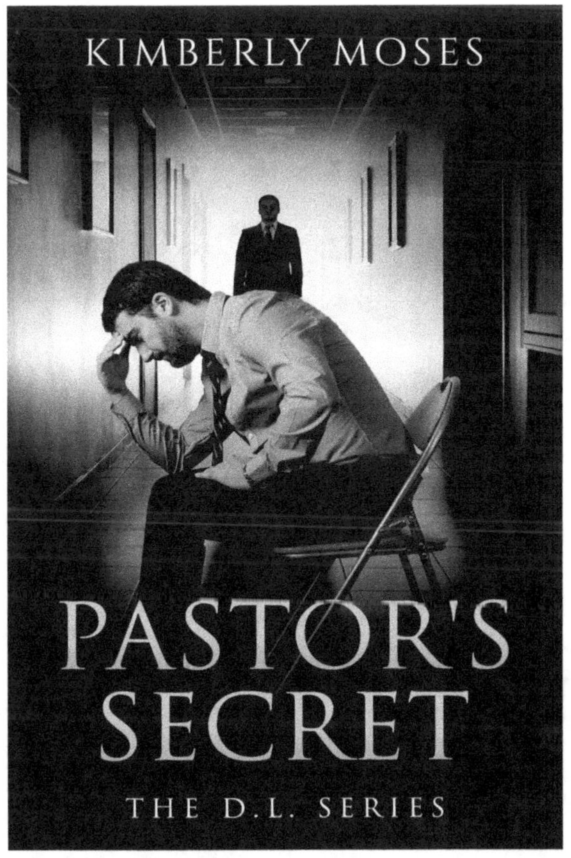

www.ingramcontent.com/pod-product-compliance
Lightning Source LLC
Chambersburg PA
CBHW071840190726
48292CB00005B/1847